CHASING
BUTTERFREE

CHASING BUTTERFREE

UNOFFICIAL ADVENTURES FOR POKÉMON GO PLAYERS

Book Three

ALex PoLan

Sky Pony Press
New York

First Edition

This is a work of fiction. Names, characters, places, and incidents are from the author's imagination, and used fictitiously.

Sky Pony Press books may be purchased in bulk at special discounts for sales promotion, corporate gifts, fund-raising, or educational purposes. Special editions can also be created to specifications. For details, contact the Special Sales Department, Sky Pony Press, 307 West 36th Street, 11th Floor, New York, NY 10018 or info@skyhorsepublishing.com.

Sky Pony® is a registered trademark of Skyhorse Publishing, Inc.®, a Delaware corporation.

Visit our website at www.skyponypress.com.

Books, authors, and more at SkyPonyPressBlog.com.

10 9 8 7 6 5 4 3 2 1

Library of Congress Cataloging-in-Publication Data is available on file.

Special thanks to Erin L. Falligant.

Cover illustration by Jarrett Williams
Cover colors by Jeremy Lawson
Cover design by Brian Peterson

Print ISBN: 978-1-5107-2204-0
Ebook ISBN: 978-1-5107-2206-4

Printed in Canada

CHAPTER 1

PokéStop!" shouted Ethan, spinning the Photo Disc on his phone. It showed a photo of the stone lion at the entrance to the Jamestown Zoo.

"What did you get?" asked Carlo, tossing the hair out of his eyes as he checked his own phone.

"Um, three Poké Balls and . . . an egg. Ooh, it's a five-kilometer egg." Ethan happily placed the egg in an incubator.

"Wait up!" shouted Ethan's younger sister, Devin. "Did you find a Pokémon already?"

"Nah, just a PokéStop," said Ethan. "But we'll start seeing Pokémon soon, I'm sure. I've heard there are Abra and Mankey here at the zoo—all kinds of rare Pokémon. Plus a ton of PokéStops!"

"Don't forget the Butterfree!" shouted Gianna, Carlo's younger sister. As she ran toward them, the bug antennae on her green cap bobbled up and down.

"You *look* like a Butterfree in that hat." Devin giggled.

"More like a Caterpie," said Carlo, playfully pushing the cap down over Gianna's eyes.

"Hey!" she shouted. "No touching. That's my lucky Pokémon-hunting cap."

"Butterfree? Caterpie? Whatever happened to butterflies and caterpillars?" asked the woman walking behind them. Her hair was as dark and curly as Gianna's.

"Sorry, Mom," said Gianna, straightening the cap on her head. "That's Pokémon language. Can I borrow your phone to play Pokémon GO?"

Her mother sighed. "For a little while," she said, fishing her phone from her tote bag. "But make sure you kids keep your eyes open for real animals, too, here at the zoo. Especially butterflies."

"Yes, Mrs. Walker," said Ethan. "And thanks for bringing us here," he added.

He hadn't been to the zoo in ages. It was an hour's drive from Newville, where he and his friends lived. But the zoo was hosting a new butter-fly exhibit, and Gianna loved bugs. Maybe it was because her mom was an entomologist—a fancy name for a bug scientist.

So because Gia and her mom love bugs, we all get to go to the zoo, thought Ethan. *How lucky can a Pokémon GO player be?*

"Don't feed the animals," Carlo read off the sign near the zoo entrance. "Do Razz Berries count?" He showed Ethan the Razz Berries he'd collected at the PokéStop.

Ethan laughed out loud. "Probably not." As he stepped through the iron gates, he was surprised to see "Pokémon GO" written on a sign on an information booth.

Gianna spotted it, too. "Look, Mom," she said, racing toward the booth. "The zoo *wants* us to play Pokémon GO. It's a scavenger hunt!"

"Awesome!" said Devin. "How does it work?"

A woman wearing an orange polo shirt with a Jamestown Zoo badge waved them over. "Just find the team stickers," she said. "Yellow for Team Instinct, red for Team Valor, and blue for—"

"Team Mystic!" Ethan said, grinning. "We know. That's us."

He and his friends had all joined Team Mystic as soon as they reached Level Five. They defended their own gym, too, at Dottie's Doughnuts in Newville.

"Good," said the zoo guide, smiling. "So you already have a head start. The stickers are given out at three stations hidden throughout the zoo. Bring the stickers back here, and you'll get a free gift from the gift shop." She pointed toward the red-brick building right behind her booth.

"Can we do it?" Gianna asked her mom.

Mrs. Walker hesitated—until the zoo guide added, "It's educational. The kids will learn something about animals at each station."

A smile spread across Mrs. Walker's face. She shrugged. "Well, if it's *educational*, how can I say no?"

"I wonder what the prize will be," said Devin, stepping toward the gift shop and pressing her freckled face against the window.

Ethan looked, too. His eyes went straight to the stuffed animals. "A stuffed boa constrictor, maybe? That purple one looks like Ekans."

"I'd take the ladybug umbrella," said Gianna. "Or one of those geodes. Aren't those the rocks that you crack open? You never know what you're going to find inside."

"Like my Pokémon Egg," said Ethan, checking his phone.

"Maybe you'll find a Geo*dude* in your geode," Gianna joked. "Get it?"

"Nah, think bigger," said Carlo. "You can get a Geodude from a two-kilometer egg. Maybe you'll get a Magnemite or a Grimer in the five-kilometer one."

Devin scrunched up her nose. "Yeah, who would want a Geodude when you could have a sticky, stinky purple blob of a Pokémon like Grimer?" she said sarcastically.

Carlo stepped backward, and then suddenly groaned.

"What's wrong?" asked Mrs. Walker.

"I think I might have just stepped on Grimer." As he lifted his foot, a string of bubble gum stretched from his shoe down to the blacktop.

As Ethan watched Carlo scrape the gum off his shoe, he checked the bottoms of his own shoes and then wiped his hands on his shorts. They suddenly felt sticky.

"Hey, let's take a photo!" said Devin, pointing toward the gift shop photo booth. "It looks like you can even wear animal masks."

Three kids were stepping out of the booth and tossing masks back into a bucket beside the booth.

"I'll take the ostrich mask," said Devin,

reaching into the bucket. She handed the panda bear to Ethan.

"There's another ostrich," said Gianna, digging the mask out of the bucket. "We can be twins!"

When she and Devin stood side by side with their masks on, Ethan chuckled. "Actually, you look like a two-headed Doduo. Except one of your heads has bug antennae."

Gianna snorted and pulled off her bug cap. "Is that better?"

"Much," he said.

They piled into the booth and waited for the camera to count down.

Five, four, three . . .

"Wait for me!" Carlo slid into the booth wearing an orangutan mask. He sat down on his sister's lap just as the flash went off in the booth.

"Get off!" she shouted. "You covered me up!"

But when Ethan reached for the photo that slid out of the slot on the side of the booth, he could see all four heads. "We're all here," he announced. "A panda, a Doduo, and an orangutan—with perfect hair."

Gianna playfully punched her brother in the shoulder. "Carlo never has a hair out of place," she teased.

"Are we ready?" asked Mrs. Walker, who was

waiting outside.

"Yes!" said Ethan. "What should we see first?"

Then he noticed that Gianna and Devin were already running toward the petting zoo.

"I think I'm a little old for that," said Carlo. "They probably don't even let fourteen-year-olds inside."

"Me, too," said Ethan. He was only ten, but he'd rather hang with Carlo than get lumped in with their younger sisters.

Then he caught sight of the baby goats, bouncing around just like puppies. And Ethan *loved* puppies. He suddenly couldn't wait to feed a goat.

The goats stood up on their hind legs on the other side of the gate, stepping all over each other to nibble food out of kids' hands. Some were tan, others reddish brown, and the smallest ones black and white.

Those are the ones I'll feed, he decided.

As Mrs. Walker poured food pellets out of a cup into Devin's hand, Ethan reached for some, too, hoping Carlo wouldn't notice. Then he squatted down and stuck his hand out right in front of a black-and-white goat. "Hurry!" he whispered. "Eat quickly, before your big brothers eat it all."

"Pokémon alert!" shouted Carlo, holding up his phone. "It's Eevee."

Ethan pulled out his own phone, but he couldn't figure out what to do with the pellets in his other hand. He tried to catch Eevee one-handed, but his Poké Balls kept shooting off into the corners of the screen.

"Is that Eevee?" asked Gianna. "Oh, it's even cuter than a baby goat."

Pretty soon, all four kids were trying to catch Eevee while four hungry goats nosed at them, wondering where all the pellets had gone.

Ethan's Poké Ball finally hit its mark, and Eevee got sucked into a Poké Ball. "Yes! Gotcha." As the stars floated up from the ball, he glanced up to see how his friends were doing.

"Whoa, Gia," he said. "Don't look now, but . . ."

Of course, she looked—and saw what Ethan saw.

Gianna was staring right into the eyes of a goat. Only this was no baby goat.

This one had horns.

And it had her lucky Pokémon-catching cap in its mouth!

"Get it back!" she hollered to Ethan. "Get my cap. Quick!"

Ethan lunged for the cap. He caught the brim with his fingertips, but the goat tugged back.

What do I do? wondered Ethan. If the goat were a Pokémon, he'd fling a Poké Ball at it. But the goat was too big for a Poké Ball. *Way* too big.

And it wasn't about to give up its new prize.

CHAPTER 2

"**A**s Ethan tightened his grip on the bug cap, the goat did, too. It chomped down harder, bending back one of the antennae.

"Stop!" Gianna shrieked, pressing her hands to her head. "You're going to ruin it!"

So Ethan stopped tugging. *Think,* he told himself. *What does the goat want even more than that cap?*

Then he remembered the food pellets in his left hand. He quickly held them out toward the goat, palm up.

When a couple of baby goats came running, Ethan raised his hand higher, right under the big goat's chin. The animal's nose twitched, and it finally lowered its head—and dropped the cap.

As the goat hungrily gobbled up the pellets, Ethan saw that Gianna had scrambled under the fence to get her cap.

"No, Gia!" her mother hollered. "Get back here!"

Ethan breathed a sigh of relief when Gianna crawled back out of the pen, her cap in hand.

"Thanks," she whispered to him as she brushed the cap off. "Blech. Goat germs."

"But is it okay?" asked Devin, dropping to her knees beside Gianna.

"I think so." Gianna pulled the cap down over her dark curls. "How does it look?"

It looked *mostly* okay. Ethan saw that one of the antennae was slightly bent. Devin seemed to notice it, too. She cocked her head, as if that would somehow straighten the antenna out. But Ethan was glad when she didn't say anything about it. She just smiled and gave Gianna a thumbs-up.

Gianna blew out a breath of relief. Then she turned to face the goat. "You're very rude," she said, shaking her finger. "Some goats have no manners."

"Some kids don't either," said Mrs. Walker, raising an eyebrow. "Kids who play Pokémon GO when they're supposed to be feeding goats."

"But, Mom!" Gianna protested. "It's my lucky cap. I caught Beedrill when I was wearing this cap. I won my first gym battle when I was wearing this cap. I don't know what I'd do without it."

"I know, I know," said her mother. "So let's get out of the range of that hungry goat."

As they left the petting zoo, Ethan gave the black-and-white baby goat one last glance. "Sorry, buddy," he said. "You kind of got robbed in the pellet department."

Then he hurried to catch up with Carlo, who was standing in front of a directory map.

"It's a PokéStop," explained Carlo, pointing at the map.

Ethan pulled out his phone, but as he swiped the Photo Disc, nothing happened. Then a pink message showed up. Your bag is full.

He groaned. "I have to dump some items."

Carlo looked over his shoulder at his list of items. "Maybe discard a few Potions and Revives," he said. "You probably won't be doing many gym battles today, but you're going to want to keep your Poké Balls and Razz Berries for capturing more Pokémon."

"Right," said Ethan. Carlo was the best Pokémon GO player in the group—a Level-Thirteen Trainer, last time Ethan had checked. So when Carlo gave a tip, Ethan usually listened. He quickly discarded a bunch of Potions and Revives.

"Hey!" shouted Devin. She was standing in the doorway to a green building labeled Rainforest Center. "Gia's lucky cap struck again. We just found our first scavenger hunt station, and it's Team Mystic!" She waved the boys toward the entrance.

Sure enough, Gia and her mom were standing inside by a table with a blue Team Mystic sign on it. As Ethan followed Carlo toward the station, he stole glances at the animals inside the glass cases lining the walls.

On one side of the room, *huge* snakes wound around tree branches and coiled at the bottom of their cages. On the other side, macaws squawked from their perches and flapped their colorful wings.

"C'mon, kids. Gather round," said the zoo guide standing by the scavenger hunt table. "My name is Blanche, the leader of Team Mystic."

Ethan met Carlo's eye and grinned. Blanche was the Team Mystic leader who appeared in the Pokémon GO game when a trainer reached Level Five. Ethan was pretty sure this woman wasn't *really* named Blanche, but it was fun to think that she might be.

"Who can tell me what Team Mystic studies?"

she asked. "Are we all about strength and power, intuition, or evolution?"

"Evolution!" shouted Devin, taking the word right out of Ethan's mouth.

"That's right," said Blanche. "Very good. And did you know that the rainforest is a hot spot for evolution?"

As she talked on about the number of different animal species in the rainforest, Ethan felt his phone vibrate. He glanced down and quickly caught a Poliwag perched on the edge of the table. *Score!*

"Ethan, pay attention to Blanche," his sister said, nudging his arm.

"I am," he mumbled. "I'm all about evolution. In fact, I'm evolving Poliwag into a Poliwhirl right now."

"Really?" Devin leaned closer so that she could see the blue, froglike Pokémon bursting out of the spinning white ball of light. "Cool."

When Poliwhirl did a little dance and bubbles came out of its backside, both Ethan and Devin cracked up.

Blanche gave them a stern glance and then said, "Well, are we ready for our Team Mystic stickers?"

The blue stickers showed the outline of Articuno, the legendary bird Pokémon. Ethan stuck his to his T-shirt, just as Devin and Gianna had. But Carlo slapped his to his forehead—until Mrs. Walker made him take it off.

After taking one loop around the glass cages to look at the birds and boa constrictors, Ethan followed the rest of the group out of the Rainforest Center. He didn't have to ask where they were going next. Mrs. Walker was practically running toward the Butterfly House.

Devin laughed. "The Butterfly House is like a petting zoo for your mom, isn't it?"

Gianna nodded. "Except there's no petting involved. You can't touch the butterflies—you'll damage the scales on their wings."

Ethan barely heard her. He had just noticed that someone had set a lure at the PokéStop outside the Butterfly House. Pink petals fell all around the blue icon on his phone screen.

When he spun the blue disc, he was surprised to see another five-kilometer egg pop up. "It's my lucky day!" he said, placing the egg in his second incubator.

"Well, it's not mine," Devin grumbled. "It says my bag is full. No fair!"

"That happened to me when we got here," he told her. "Just get rid of some stuff." But he knew she wouldn't listen. Devin couldn't get rid of *anything.* He'd had a hard time convincing her to trade in some Pidgey for Pidgey Candy once, too.

"That's okay," she said, sliding her phone into her pocket. "I'll just enjoy the butterflies."

"Attagirl," said Mrs. Walker, who was standing at the entrance to the Butterfly House. "Come on, kids!"

Ethan waited for Carlo. "Did you see the lure?" he asked.

"Yeah," said Carlo, "and I'm hot on the trail of a Venomoth. This place is packed with Pokémon!" He pumped his fist as the Venomoth on his screen was swallowed up by a Great Ball.

By the time Ethan made it through the first set of glass doors into the Butterfly House, he had already caught a Bellsprout and a Kakuna.

"Don't let any butterflies escape," the exhibit guide was saying. "Make sure one set of doors is closed before you open the other."

Ethan put his phone down to show that he was paying attention. As he stepped through the second door, he felt as if he'd just walked into a tropical wonderland.

Sun streamed through the windows at the top of the Butterfly House. Lush green plants grew beside the stream that wound alongside the stone walkway. And colorful butterflies dipped and dove gracefully around him.

"Watch your step," said Mrs. Walker, her eyes gleaming. "And if a butterfly lands on you, remember not to touch it!" She led the way down the path, looking up, down, and all around.

Just a few feet ahead of Ethan, Devin stopped suddenly. "Gia, there's a butterfly on your shoulder!" she whispered, raising her phone to take a picture.

Ethan could just make out the orange butterfly, which seemed perfectly content hitching a ride on Gianna.

She tilted her head, trying to see sideways. "Is it orange? I think that's a Queen butterfly." She checked the brochure she must have grabbed at the exhibit entrance while Devin tried to get the perfect shot.

"Smile!" said Devin.

Ethan wasn't sure whether she was talking to Gianna or to the butterfly.

Then Devin stopped to read one of the informational signs out loud. "Hey, Ethan, did you know that some butterflies are nearly invisible? Their colors blend in with their surroundings, like camo . . ."

"Camouflage?" he said. "Yeah, I think I knew that."

Every few steps, she stopped to read another sign. Ethan wished he could empty out her item bag himself so that she'd start playing Pokémon GO again instead of playing Butterfly House tour guide.

He hurried past Devin toward the bridge crossing the small stream. Mrs. Walker pointed to the orange-and-white fish swimming below, which looked like giant goldfish. "See those, Ethan? They're Japanese koi. Aren't they beautiful?"

That's when Ethan's phone vibrated and he saw the Pokémon on his screen. "Goldeen! No way!"

"Where? I don't have that one yet!" said Gianna, hurrying to catch up. She bent over the bridge, waiting for Goldeen to show up on her screen.

"Gia, for heaven's sakes, don't fall!" said her mother. "And don't you dare drop anything into the water—especially my phone."

"I won't. But where's Goldeen?" Gianna asked. She checked the other side of the bridge and bent herself into pretzels until she finally found the Pokémon.

"Gotcha!" Ethan heard her call, just as he scooped up the Pokémon with his own ball.

As he straightened back up, he heard Devin whisper to him. It sounded like she was standing just a few inches away. "*Don't* move, Ethan. There's a ginormous blue butterfly on your head."

A shiver ran down his spine. "What kind of butterfly?" he whispered back.

"You wouldn't believe it if I told you," she said. "Let me get a picture."

He heard the *snap* of her phone, which must have startled the butterfly. When Ethan felt the flutter of wings, he glanced up. Then he immediately ducked—he couldn't help it!

It was the biggest butterfly he'd ever seen.

And it had just been sitting on *his* head.

CHAPTER 3

"It's so big!" said Devin, showing Ethan and Gianna the picture of the butterfly.

"And so blue," said Gianna, her eyes sparkling. "I've read about the Blue Morpho butterfly before, but I've never seen one. It doesn't even look real. It looks more like a Pokémon, doesn't it?"

"Oh, it's *very* real," said Mrs. Walker, rubbing her hands together as if she'd just received a great gift. "We don't have them up here in the States. They live in tropical rainforests. We're lucky to see one here today."

"And Ethan was lucky enough to have it land right on him," said Carlo, reaching over to pat

Ethan's head.

"Hey!" said Ethan. "Don't touch the hair." He pretended to smooth it back in place, the way Carlo would.

Then Ethan caught sight of something along the path ahead. A small table was set up with a very yellow sign on it. He recognized it immediately as Team Instinct yellow.

"It's another scavenger hunt station!" he said. "C'mon!"

The station was set up next to a tall wooden cabinet labeled Chrysalis Case. As Ethan got closer, he saw what was inside: row upon row of butterfly pupae, hanging from long sticks.

"Are those real?" he asked the exhibit guide, a gray-haired man with thick glasses.

"Indeed," said the man. "My name is Spark, and I'm the leader of Team Instinct. We study Pokémon intuition, and I'm pretty sure it's related to how Pokémon are *hatched*."

"Ha! Get it?" said Mrs. Walker as she stepped up behind Ethan. "Pokémon hatch from eggs. Butterflies emerge from a pupa, or a chrysalis. That's very clever."

"Well, thank you," said Spark with a smile, as if he'd written the scavenger-hunt script himself. "Does anyone know how long it might take for a butterfly to 'hatch' from a pupa?"

Gianna raised her hand. "About two weeks," she said. "At least that's what Mom told me once."

"Very good. You, young lady, earn a sticker." Spark handed her a yellow sticker, which she stuck to her tank top right next to the blue one.

He gave stickers to the rest of the kids and even to Mrs. Walker, who laughed and stuck it to her tote bag. Ethan noticed that this sticker was in the shape of Zapdos, another legendary, birdlike Pokémon—and also the Team Instinct mascot.

"Only one more station to go!" he said to his friends. "We're looking for Team Valor now."

At the very mention of Team Valor, Devin turned around and scrunched up her freckled nose.

Ethan felt the same way. Team Valor was the rival team—and defenders of a rival gym—back home in Newville.

"Hey, it looks like a butterfly is coming out!" said Gianna, pointing toward the Chrysalis Case.

Sure enough, Ethan could see little butterfly legs poking through a slit in the chrysalis. He and his friends watched for a while, but it was slow going for that poor butterfly. When Ethan turned around, he saw that he and his friends were holding up a whole line of people.

Mrs. Walker must have just noticed it, too.

"Let's keep moving, kids," she said quickly. "It can take a long time for a butterfly to emerge from a chrysalis."

That's when Ethan remembered his Pokémon Egg. *Is my Pokémon going to hatch anytime soon?* he wondered. He checked the numbers next to the egg.

Nope. He had walked only a single kilometer so far. *Hopefully it won't be like a butterfly and take two weeks,* he thought with a sigh.

"Hey, Ethan, did you know that adult butterflies never eat? They only drink nectar from flowers."

Devin was beside him again, stopping to read every single sign she saw out loud.

Great.

"Hey, Ethan, did you know that butterflies smell with their antennae?"

He kept walking.

"Hey, Ethan, did you know you have a butterfly on your butt?"

That one got his attention.

"Where?" he asked, freezing mid-step. "Is it another Blue Morpho?"

"No," said Devin. "This one is a lot smaller. Turn around and see for yourself."

As he slowly twisted around, he caught sight of

a little black-and-white butterfly. It reminded him of the baby goat at the petting zoo.

"That's a Zebra butterfly," said Gianna, checking her brochure. "He's so cute!"

"Yeah, but what do I do with him?" asked Ethan. "Should I start walking?"

"Wait!" said Devin. "Let me get a picture first. I'm going to frame this photo and call it 'Butterfly.' Because it's on your butt, get it?"

Ethan groaned. "That's a Dad joke," he said. "You're about as funny as he is."

Devin stuck out her tongue, but her eyes were smiling.

As soon as he started walking again, Ethan was relieved to see the Zebra butterfly flutter away overhead. But as they neared the end of the exhibit, Ethan took a good, long look in the floor-length mirror to make sure he didn't have any other "butt-erflies" on his backside.

A sign posted above the door read, CHECK YOURSELF IN THE MIRROR. DO A BUTTERFLY DANCE TO GENTLY SHAKE OFF ANY BUTTERFLIES BEFORE LEAVING.

"A butterfly dance?" said Devin. "I can do that."

She started fluttering her wings in the air, and pretty soon Gianna was doing it, too.

"Wait for me, Carlo," Ethan called as Carlo disappeared through the exit door. "The girls are taking this butterfly dance thing a little too far."

As Ethan closed the glass door, he made sure no butterflies came with him.

"Where to next?" he asked Carlo, who was hitting up the PokéStop out front for more Poké Balls.

"It looks like there are more PokéStops near the Polar Passage," said Carlo, checking the map on his phone. "And maybe a polar bear, too!"

So as soon as the girls and Mrs. Walker stepped outside, Ethan and Carlo led the way to the Polar Passage.

As they passed the seal tank, Ethan watched a spotted seal do a somersault in the water before swimming away. He checked his phone, hoping to spot a Seel there, too. He didn't have one of those yet! But no such luck.

"PokéStop!" called Carlo. He was standing beside a statue of a polar bear rising up on its hind legs.

Ethan hurried over and racked up a few Poké Balls, too, trying not to think about how scary a real polar bear might be if it were standing beside him. *Those things are tall!* he realized.

"Oh, there's the polar bear!" shouted Devin, which made Ethan jump.

He followed her gaze toward the entrance to the polar bear cave. "Where?"

"You missed it," she said. "You were too busy looking at your phone."

Ethan sighed. He wished he'd seen the polar bear, but he also wished he'd see some Pokémon sometime soon. "Where did all the Pokémon go?" he asked out loud.

Carlo shrugged. "I don't know. I haven't seen one since the Butterfly House."

"And I'm wearing my lucky cap and everything," said Gianna, searching her own phone screen.

"Wait a second. No, you're not," said Mrs. Walker.

"What?"

When he heard the panic in Gianna's voice, Ethan whirled around. Sure enough, her head was bare. She spun in a circle, searching the ground.

"I lost my lucky cap!" she shouted. "We have to find it. We have to go back. Now!"

CHAPTER 4

Gia, wait!" shouted Mrs. Walker.

But Gianna's dark curls had already disappeared around the corner of the seal exhibit.

"I'll catch her," said Carlo, taking off after his sister.

Ethan followed close behind, wishing he were wearing his new sneakers. He'd never seen Gia run so fast!

They caught up to her just outside the Butterfly House. She was rushing to get in, but a cluster of people at the entrance were blocking her path.

"Please," she said, a panic-stricken look on her face. "I have to get inside!"

Ethan recognized the gray-haired man with the thick glasses who stood in Gianna's way. It was Spark!

"I'm afraid there's been an escape," he explained to Gia. "A butterfly just got out of the exhibit. But if we could all keep our voices down and search quietly, we might be able to find it."

"What?" cried Mrs. Walker, who had finally caught up to them. "What kind of butterfly?" She looked as upset about the butterfly as Gia did about her lost cap.

Spark sighed. "A Blue Morpho. One of the largest and rarest ones."

Devin sucked in her breath, and Mrs. Walker's face fell. "Oh, dear. What bad luck."

"See?" said Gianna, spreading her arms wide. "It's because I lost my lucky cap. We have to find it!" As soon as someone came out of the Butterfly House, she pushed her way in.

"I see the Morpho!" someone shouted from the edge of the crowd.

As Mrs. Walker's eyes lit up, Carlo stepped toward the entrance. "You help find the butterfly, Mom," he said. "We'll help Gia find her cap."

Mrs. Walker nodded. "Stay together. Do not

split up. Do you hear me, Carlo?"

He nodded, ran his hand over his dark hair, and ducked into the entrance.

"Hurry, Ethan," said Devin. "Follow him. We have to help Gia!"

When Ethan hesitated too long, she pushed past him and tried to get through the door, too. But the Butterfly House exhibit guides were making sure people entered one at a time.

"We don't want to lose any more butterflies," said the dark-haired woman in the orange shirt who finally let Ethan in.

By then, he couldn't see his friends anywhere. *So much for not splitting up!* he thought. He hurried along the stone path, making sure not to step on any butterflies.

This time, he paid attention to every sign he passed in the exhibit—at least to scan the signs for a green bug cap with yellow antennae. Had Gianna taken it off and hung it somewhere?

When his phone vibrated to tell him a Pokémon or PokéStop was nearby, he ignored it, though it took all his willpower. And he hurried faster along the trail—past the bridge over the stream, past the Chrysalis Case, and finally to the mirrors at the exit.

Gianna, Carlo, and Devin were all waiting

there. And Ethan could tell by the looks on their faces that they hadn't found the cap, either.

"Where could it be?" asked Gianna.

When Ethan saw tears welling up in her eyes, he tried to think of something to say that would make her feel better. "I don't know, Gia, but we'll find it. It's just another mystery to solve, and we're good at solving mysteries, remember?"

Devin nodded. "We are! We found Mrs. Applegate's cat. And a cat is a whole lot harder to find than a cap."

Gianna wiped her nose and laughed. "That's true."

"So is Team Mystic on the case?" asked Ethan. He held out his hand, palm down.

"Team Mystic," said Devin, putting her hand on top.

Carlo and Gianna added their hands, too. "Team Mystic."

"Good," said Ethan, straightening back up. "So maybe we should retrace our steps. Which exhibit were we at before this one? Let's think!"

"The petting zoo?" asked Devin. "No, wait, the Rainforest Center!"

Gianna's face brightened. Then she pushed open the exit door and took off.

Ethan took a quick look in the mirror to make

sure his body—especially his butt—was free of butterflies. Then he followed his teammates out the door.

"Hello, kids. My name is Blanche, and I'm the leader of Team Mystic."

They had just stepped into the Rainforest Center, and it was as if the lady at the scavenger hunt station had never seen them before!

"We were already here, Blanche," said Ethan, trying not to sound impatient. "See?" He pulled out the front of his T-shirt to show her the Team Mystic sticker she had given him just an hour or two earlier.

"Oh, sorry!" said Blanche, shrugging. "I meet a lot of kids, you know."

"No worries," said Carlo, who sounded much more calm than Ethan felt. "Have you seen a green bug cap, by chance? With antennae on top?"

"I sure did," said Blanche. "There it is right now!" She pointed toward the doorway, where a couple of kids were walking out. A girl with a long blonde braid was wearing a green cap—a cap with *antennae* on top!

"Follow that cap!" shouted Ethan. He couldn't

believe their good luck! They'd caught the thief red-handed.

But as he ran toward the door, a group of kids in matching tie-dyed T-shirts piled into the Rainforest Center and charged toward Blanche and the Team Mystic table. Ethan tried to dodge around them and get to the door. But it was like swimming upstream. He finally had to stand still and let them run around him.

By the time he and his friends made it out of the Rainforest Center, the bug cap was nowhere in sight.

"So someone *stole* it?" said Gianna, her eyes wide. "I can't believe someone would do that!"

"Whoever stole it is probably going to catch some good Pokémon," said Carlo, checking his phone. "Because I haven't caught a single one since you lost that cap."

"Me neither," said Ethan with a sigh.

"Forget about the Pokémon, already," said Devin, shading her eyes. "I think I see Gia's cap." She pointed toward a bunch of little kids lined up by a sign that read Zoo Train.

Ethan spotted the green bug cap, too. The blonde girl wearing it was the tallest kid in line!

"Let's go!" he shouted.

Ethan and Carlo reached the line first and tried

to weave their way through it, toward the blonde girl.

"Hey, no cutting!" shouted a short kid in a striped shirt.

"My friend lost her cap," Ethan tried to explain. "Someone up there stole it!"

"Really?" said the kid, his eyes wide. But as he stepped aside to let Ethan pass, someone else in striped overalls moved into his place.

The zoo guide dressed like a train conductor held up his hand. "Sorry, kids," he said. "This train is full. You'll have to take the next one."

He pointed toward a second train coming down the tracks. It slowed to a halt with a puff of steam.

"We don't want to take the train," Ethan managed to say. "We're trying to stop it!"

He pointed toward the first train. The girl wearing Gianna's cap had her head out the window, with one antenna bouncing off the top of the train.

For just a second, Ethan thought about charging the train and yanking the cap off her head. But before he could make up his mind about what to do, the train started chugging down the tracks. *Too late,* he thought.

"This way, folks," said the conductor, shepherding Ethan and Carlo toward the second train.

Ethan tried to step aside, but the line of kids behind him pushed him and Carlo forward—especially the little kid in the striped shirt.

"What are we doing?" he heard Devin cry from behind.

As he looked over his shoulder and met her eyes, he shrugged.

"I guess we're getting on the train."

He felt another push from behind and stumbled forward.

CHAPTER 5

Sitting in that train, Carlo looked like a gorilla riding in a clown car. He ducked his head low to avoid hitting it against the roof of the train car—or maybe to make sure he didn't mess up his hair. And he had his knees tucked way up under his chin.

"Don't laugh," he warned Ethan. "This is so not funny. And Devin, don't you dare take a picture."

But Ethan's chest started shaking with laughter. And Devin had a full-blown case of the giggles.

"Hey, he's right!" grumbled Gianna, who had

her own head stuck out the window. "This isn't funny. Some girl stole my cap, and her train is faster than ours!"

Ethan *tried* to stop laughing. But looking at his friends—any one of them—didn't help matters. Carlo looked ridiculous. Gia practically had steam coming out of her ears, she was so mad. And Devin's giggles were contagious.

So he pulled out his phone to look for Pokémon. What else was he supposed to do? And there, right in front of his eyes, was a Mankey!

The monkeylike Pokémon was round and brown, with angry eyes. And it was sitting on Carlo's shoulder.

When Ethan raised his phone, Carlo put his hand up. "Do not take a picture!" he said. "I told you!"

"I'm not," said Ethan, holding the phone and his voice steady. "There's a Mankey in here. And I'm about to make it mine." He waited until the Pokémon did its dodge move. Then Ethan flung a Poké Ball directly at the Mankey.

It was a great shot—straight and high!

But it *froze* in midair.

"No!" Ethan shouted, shaking his phone.

He'd lost the signal.

"No!"

He restarted the app, but the Mankey was long gone. And as the train headed around a bend in the tracks, Ethan's screen froze up again. He sighed and dropped the phone in his lap.

"Man, we really *are* having bad luck," he muttered.

Gianna pulled her head back into the train and gave him The Look—the one that pretty much said, "Really? Do you think so? Are you just figuring that out now?"

So he zipped his lips and kept quiet for the rest of the train ride. He hoped they'd catch up with the first train eventually, but that one chugged steadily along the track and only seemed to be getting farther ahead.

The two trains passed by a fenced-in prairie filled with huge bison. They crossed a rickety bridge over a sparkling stream. Then, *finally*, they seemed to be curving back around to where they started from. Only a short stone tunnel lay between the trains and the station.

Ethan watched as the train up ahead chugged into the tunnel, popped back out of the other side, and then came to a stop at the station. As kids spilled out of the train, he spotted the green bug cap. He tried to keep his eyes fixed on it as the blonde girl stepped back into the crowd of kids.

But then Ethan's own train entered the tunnel, and everything went black.

"Maybe we should tell someone," said Devin after they'd gotten off the train. "Like at an information booth. Can't the zoo people track down the thief and make her give your hat back?"

Gianna shrugged. "They probably won't believe us."

"Sure they will!" said Devin.

While Carlo stretched out his legs, Ethan stood on tiptoe, hoping he could spot the green cap in the crowd of people ahead. But the blonde girl was long gone.

"We might as well tell someone," he said. "What do we have to lose?"

As soon as the words left his mouth, he realized something. Since Gianna had lost her cap, they'd lost a lot of *other* things, too: a phone signal, a Mankey, and even a Morpho butterfly. *So at this rate, our luck could get a whole lot worse before it gets better,* he reminded himself.

But Carlo was already on his way to the nearest information booth. By the time Ethan got there, Carlo was telling the zoo guide what had happened. The man in the orange polo wrote down all of the information, and Gianna even drew a picture of the cap for him on the back of a zoo map.

"Anything else you can think of that might be helpful?" the man asked.

When they shook their heads, he reached for his phone and made a few calls. Every time Ethan heard him say the words "We have a lost cap," he wanted to correct the man. *It's not lost. It was stolen!*

Gianna looked as if she were biting her tongue, too.

Then the zoo guide said something that caught everyone's attention.

"You see the cap?" he said into the phone. "Really? Okay, we'll be right there!"

He propped up a CLOSED sign on his booth and stepped out the side doorway. "C'mon, kids," he said. "We may have found your cap."

They followed him past the Rainforest Center, past the Butterfly House, past the Polar Passage, and toward the zoo playground. A giant giraffe slide towered over the other playground equipment. There, beside a blue teeter-totter shaped like a seal, Ethan saw another zoo guide dressed in orange. She waved to them and hurried over.

"Which one of you lost the cap?" she asked.

Gianna raised her hand. "Me. I did."

"Okay," said the guide, crouching beside Gianna. "Is that your cap?" She pointed toward a girl leaning against the playground fence.

Sure enough, it was the girl with the long blonde braid—and she was still wearing Gia's cap!

Gianna shaded her eyes against the sun. "Yeah, that's mine!" She chewed nervously on her fingernail. "Can you get it back for me?"

The zoo guide nodded. "I think so. We can have a chat with the girl, at least, and see what's what."

As she crossed the playground, Ethan's heart raced. He couldn't believe they were confronting the thief. She was *so* busted! Part of him wanted to look the other way, he was so nervous. The other part of him wished he had a pair of handcuffs to slap on her wrists himself.

As the guide started talking to the girl, Ethan saw her face crumple. She shook her head no and grabbed the cap. Was she going to make a run for it?

Nope. She followed the guide back across the playground.

As they got closer, he could see that the girl's cheeks were splotchy with embarrassment.

"She says she got the cap at the gift shop," said the zoo guide.

"But she didn't!" said Ethan, his voice rising. "We were already at the gift shop. They don't sell caps like that." *What a liar!* he wanted to add.

But Gianna held up her hand to stop him. "Maybe they do," she said in a small voice.

Huh?

"That's not my cap," said Gianna sadly. "The antennae are the wrong color."

Ethan took a closer look at the cap—and swallowed hard. Instead of yellow antennae, this one had orange antennae. It looked even more like a Caterpie.

So that meant that the girl they'd chased half-way around the zoo was no thief.

And now she was starting to cry.

CHAPTER 6

I'm really sorry," said Gianna to the girl with the blonde braid. "Your cap looks so much like mine, but . . . it's not. I should have looked closer before I accused you of taking it. I'm sorry."

The girl sniffled and nodded.

Ethan stepped forward to apologize, too. But the girl was already hurrying back toward her friends. She had one hand pressed tightly against her cap so that it wouldn't fall off.

Or get taken away by a bunch of crazy strangers, thought Ethan sadly. His own cheeks burned hot with embarrassment now.

"Do you want to check the Lost and Found for

your cap?" the zoo guide asked Gianna.

She shrugged. She didn't look too hopeful, Ethan noticed. And he couldn't blame her. Things were going from bad to worse.

"There's a Lost and Found bin at the gift shop," the guide said. "If you can't find your old one there, maybe you can buy yourself a new one." He winked at Gianna.

Ethan knew the guide was trying to be nice. He also knew that Gia wasn't having any of it. She grumbled all the way to the gift shop.

"Seriously? He thinks I can just replace my lucky cap?" She shook her head. *"Grown ups."* She said that last part as if it were a swear word.

When they reached the gift shop, Carlo asked the cashier about the Lost and Found. He nodded and slid a big plastic bin out from under the counter.

As Gia picked and poked through the lost items, Ethan held his breath. The bin was full of hats, backpacks, stuffed animals, and shoes.

How do you lose a shoe and not know it? he wondered.

But he could tell pretty quickly that the cap wasn't in the bin. So he started scavenging the store, looking for the Caterpie cap that the blonde girl insisted she'd bought here.

Maybe I can buy one for Gia, he thought, even though he wasn't sure she'd want it.

Ethan scanned aisles full of T-shirts, stuffed animals, and animal puppets. He poked through animal purses, jewelry, and key chains. He even passed a bin full of tiny plastic animals, making a mental note to keep Devin away from that. A collector like her would want one of each of them!

As Ethan finished searching the very last aisle, he scratched his head. No Caterpie caps. So the blonde girl wasn't a thief . . . but was she a liar?

He wondered whether he should tell Team Mystic about this latest development. But Gianna looked miserable enough, and Carlo was already waving them out of the gift shop.

"We'd better let Mom know where we are," he said, pulling out his phone. After sending a quick text, he asked, "Now what? Any ideas for where to look next?"

"I guess we just have to start all over," said Gianna, dragging her feet as they walked.

Or we look for Pokémon, thought Ethan. His phone had just buzzed, and he had a strong signal! It was only a Weedle that had popped up on his screen—one of his least-favorite Pokémon. But at least it was something.

"Ethan!" Devin whispered. "You shouldn't be

playing when Gianna is upset. We need to make her feel better." Then she caught up to Gianna and took her by the arm. "Look, Gia, do you see the ostrich?"

I'm just going to catch this real quick. Then I'll stop, Ethan told himself. But there was nothing quick about capturing the Weedle.

It sprang out of the first Poké Ball like a jack-in-the-box. "Seriously, Larry?" he said, capturing it again.

"Larry" was the nickname his dad had given a Weedle once. So now Ethan and Devin called every Weedle they caught Larry.

This particular Larry bounced out of the second Poké Ball, too—and promptly disappeared with a *poof!*

"Man, why does everything feel so hard now?" Ethan said out loud, sliding his phone back into his pocket. When all three of his friends gave him the same familiar look, he raised his hand. "I know, I know: it's because Gianna lost her lucky cap. So let's find it."

He glanced around, looking for fresh ideas. That's when his eyes fell on the ostrich.

"Where's the other half of the Doduo?" he joked, pretending to look for a second ostrich. When no one laughed, he tried to explain it. "You know, like in the photo booth, remember?" But his voice kind of trailed off. Jokes weren't all that funny if you had to actually *explain* them.

He could usually count on Devin to laugh, but she wasn't even listening. She had stopped walking and was staring off into the distance, a faraway look on her face.

"What?" Ethan asked her. "Was my joke that bad? Did it send you into a trance or something?" He snapped his fingers in front of her face.

She blinked and said, "No, I was just thinking about the photo booth. Did Gia take off her cap and leave it inside?"

Carlo cocked his head. "Someone would have found it in there by now and turned it in to the Lost and Found, don't you think? And it wasn't there, remember?"

"Maybe they would have turned it in," said Ethan slowly. "Unless they thought it was just another photo prop, like the animal masks. It could be there."

"Only one way to find out!" said Gianna. She sprang into the air like a Weedle from a Poké Ball and started running back down the path.

Gianna was the first one to reach the photo booth.

Ethan crossed his fingers on both hands, hoping the cap would be inside. But just as he reached the booth, she stepped back out.

And she wasn't smiling.

"Nope," she said. "Not there. Just another dead end."

Ethan sighed. He sat on a bench next to her, and pretty soon Carlo and Devin plunked down beside them, too.

When Ethan saw that Devin had her phone out, he pretended to scold her. "No playing Pokémon GO at a time like this!" he squawked, sounding like a macaw in the Rainforest Center.

Devin rolled her eyes. "I'm not *playing*," she said. "The photo booth gave me the idea to check my photos. There might be some clues in them about the lost cap. At least the pictures will remind us where we've been today so we can retrace our steps."

"Oh, good idea." Ethan watched over her shoulder as she scrolled from picture to picture. When she reached one of the big goat with horns, he shrank backward.

But Devin seemed pretty excited about that photo. "The petting zoo!" she said. "Remember that nasty old goat that wanted to eat Gia's cap?"

I remember, alright, thought Ethan. *I'm the one*

who had to play tug-of-war with it.

So when Devin suggested they go back to the petting zoo to look for Gia's cap, Ethan didn't exactly jump for joy.

"But we got the cap *back* from the goat," he protested. "Remember?"

Devin shrugged. "Maybe Gia dropped it as we were leaving the petting zoo. Or maybe the goat lifted it off her head and she didn't even notice."

Gianna crossed her arms. "If that rude goat ate my lucky Pokémon-catching cap, I'm going to be so mad," she said.

"I'm pretty sure it didn't," said Carlo, reaching for her hand to pull her up. "But let's go visit that old goat, just in case."

They started running, but the petting zoo seemed farther away than Ethan remembered.

Devin seemed to be dragging, too, as she jogged along beside him. "I feel like we already ran five miles today!" she said, breathing hard.

Or at least five kilometers, Ethan thought suddenly. He stopped running and pulled out his phone.

"Ethan, come on!" Devin shouted over her shoulder.

He waved her on. "I'll catch up to you," he said. "I have to check something." Then he went to his

Pokémon collection and tapped on "Eggs."

They hadn't quite run five kilometers yet today, because the egg hadn't hatched. "But we ran two and a half kilometers!" he said out loud, checking the numbers by his incubating egg.

He sprinted after his sister, determined to cover the last two and a half kilometers as quickly as he could.

"Wait up!" he called to Devin.

He veered right at the petting zoo and nearly ran into a rope that had been strung across the entrance. A CLOSED sign dangled from the rope. But he could hear Devin's voice coming from somewhere nearby. Where was she?

He shaded his eyes and looked into the petting zoo. There she was! Devin was standing by the wooden fence with Gianna and Carlo—and about a million baby goats.

Why are they inside the petting zoo if it's closed? Ethan wondered. He almost called out to Devin, but he didn't want to get his friends in trouble. So he looked both ways to see if any of the zoo guides were around, and then he stepped over the rope.

As he approached the wooden fence, none of his friends looked up to greet him, but the goats sure did.

"Sorry, little guys. I'm fresh out of pellets," he

whispered. Then he asked Devin, "What are you doing in here? Didn't you see that the petting zoo is closed?"

Devin didn't say a word. She just pointed.

There, in the far corner of the goat pen, was the rude old goat—the big one with horns. He was nibbling at something round. Something flat. Something *green*.

As Ethan squinted to get a better look, he heard Gia sniffling beside him.

"So much for my lucky cap," she said quietly. "It's gone now."

CHAPTER 7

"**M**aybe we can distract the goat long enough to get in there and rescue Gia's cap," said Carlo, pacing back and forth in front of the wooden fence. "Do we have enough money for those little food pellets?"

"Sure," said Gia. "But there's no one at the pellet stand to buy them from. The petting zoo is closed, remember?"

"Right," said Carlo.

"Wait—there are pellet machines. Look!" said Devin, pointing. She hurried toward one of the machines. "Does anyone have any quarters?"

Ethan dug in his pockets and found only the

two ten-dollar bills his mom had given him for souvenirs. "Will the machine accept PokéCoins?" he joked. But that joke fell flat, just like the last one. "Sorry," he whispered to no one in particular.

"Wait, here's one!" said Devin, crouching beneath the machine. She picked up a coin from the ground, quickly wiped it off, and slid it in the slot.

The sound of the knob cranking on the pellet machine brought the goats running—*all* of them.

"It's working!" said Ethan as he watched the big goat trot toward the fence. "He dropped Gia's hat. He's coming this way! But, wait, now what do we do?"

He was surprised to see that Carlo already had a plan in place. As the goat ran toward the fence, Carlo started running *around* the fence.

"Is he going to climb into the goat pen?" asked Ethan, sucking in his breath.

Gia's eyes grew wide. "I think so. You don't think that goat will hurt him, do you?"

Ethan shrugged. "I sure wouldn't mess with the goat," he said, watching the animal knock all the little goats out of the way to get to the pellets in Devin's hand.

But the pellets didn't last very long. As soon as they were gone, Ethan looked up to see how Carlo was doing.

"Oh, no," he said under his breath. Carlo was sprinting across the back of the goat pen, racing toward Gia's cap. But when the goats saw him running, they started to run, too!

The little ones ran away into the corner of the pen.

But the big goat set his sights on Carlo—and ran *toward* him.

"Hurry!" said Ethan, forgetting to keep his voice down. "Get out of there, Carlo!"

But Carlo seemed determined to get Gia's cap. He slipped in something and nearly wiped out, but he managed to touch his hand to the ground and push himself back up.

When he finally reached the cap, he grabbed it and turned to sprint the other way. Then he stopped in his tracks and stared down at the cap.

He muttered something that Ethan couldn't hear. Then he flung the cap to the ground and ran back toward the fence.

"My cap!" Gianna cried. "Why'd he drop it?"

Ethan couldn't answer her. He couldn't speak at all—not until Carlo made it out of that pen alive. He watched his friend dive over the wooden fence just as the big goat reached it.

The goat climbed up two rungs, as if he might leap the fence, too. But he didn't. He just stared down at Carlo, who had fallen to the ground. Then the goat turned his head and started chewing something, as if he were now bored of chasing him.

Ethan raced around the fence toward Carlo, who was breathing hard as he pushed himself off the ground. Before Ethan could ask if he was okay, Gianna started shouting.

"Why did you leave my cap in there, Carlo?" she asked, her hands on her hips. "You climb into a pen filled with wild animals, you actually get my cap, and then you *drop* it? I don't understand!"

Carlo shrugged. "They're not exactly wild animals," he said. "And it wasn't your cap, Gia. It was just some dusty old rubber ball that was popped and full of goat spit."

His words hung in the air for a moment.

Then Gianna dropped her hands to her sides. "Oh."

"Did you hurt yourself?" asked Devin, giving Carlo the once-over.

He grimaced. "I think I slipped on goat poop," he said. "But I'm okay."

Gia's cheek started to twitch. Ethan was afraid she was going to cry, but she didn't—she laughed out loud instead.

"First, you stepped in bubble gum," she said,

covering her mouth with her hand. "Now, goat poop. My bad luck is sure rubbing off on you, Carlo. I can't wait to tell Mom about this one!"

Ethan was glad to see that she was smiling again. *If I'd known all it would take was a little goat poop, I would have stepped in some a long time ago!* he thought with a grin.

"You don't *have* to tell Mom about this," said Carlo. "Actually, wait. Has she texted us back yet?" He pulled the phone from his pocket. "She hasn't. That's so weird. Is she still looking for that butterfly?"

"I don't know," said Gianna. "Maybe you should call her."

Carlo punched in the number and then raised the phone to his ear. But when another phone rang nearby, everyone froze.

"Is she already here somewhere?" asked Carlo, whirling around.

"Ah, no," said Gianna with an embarrassed chuckle. She slowly slid the ringing phone from her pocket.

"Uh-oh," said Carlo. "We've had Mom's phone this whole time?"

Gianna nodded, and then her smile was gone.

"If she couldn't get a hold of us," said Carlo, running his hand over his hair, "she's probably really worried. She won't know where we are."

"She's going to be worried and *mad*," Gianna whispered. "We've gotta get back to that Butterfly House. Let's go!"

"Hold it right there," a man's voice boomed. "What's going on in here? Didn't you kids see that the petting zoo is closed?"

A man in an orange shirt was walking toward the goat pen. And he didn't look happy—not at all.

Uh-oh is right, thought Ethan, swallowing hard. He wished he could follow the baby goats right into the corner of the pen and hide.

CHAPTER 8

"Carlo tried to explain why they were in the petting zoo, but the man in orange wasn't listening.

"Closed means closed," he said, leading Ethan and his friends back toward the entrance gate. He stopped right by the CLOSED sign and pointed at each letter, one by one, as if he were standing in front of a classroom teaching them how to read.

The man's zoo badge read EARL SWEET. *But he's about as sweet as that old goat in the pen*, thought Ethan.

He hoped Mr. Sweet would let them go free after a good scolding. Instead, the guide asked the dreaded question: "Where are your parents?"

Carlo stepped forward. "Our mom is, um, at the Butterfly House," he said.

"Call her, please," said Mr. Sweet. "I'd like to have a word with your mom."

Carlo stuffed his hands in his pockets and hung his head. "We can't actually do that, sir," he said. "See, she doesn't have her phone—we do. We accidentally brought it with us when we split up."

Oh, man, thought Ethan. Everything that came out of Carlo's mouth sounded like a made-up excuse, even though it was all true!

So that was how they ended up walking *with* Mr. Sweet to the Butterfly House.

Mrs. Walker was standing out front with a scowl on her face. And when she saw that the kids were being led to the Butterfly House by an angry zoo guide, the furrow in her forehead got even deeper.

Carlo turned around. "Brace yourself," he whispered. "We're in for it now."

"So let me get this straight," said Mrs. Walker later, when they were sitting around a wooden table in the picnic area. "You chased a girl all over the zoo and accused her of stealing Gia's cap, but it was the *wrong* cap. You broke into the petting zoo when it was closed to try to save Gia's cap, but you saved an old ball covered in goat drool instead. Oh, and then Carlo stepped in goat poop. Does that about sum it up?"

Her mouth twitched. Ethan was pretty sure she was trying not to smile.

"Yeah," said Carlo. "That about sums it up."

"Did you find the Morpho butterfly, Mrs. Walker?" asked Devin.

She's trying to change the subject, Ethan realized.

But Mrs. Walker sighed. "No, we couldn't find the butterfly anywhere. It's probably long gone by now."

"What a *terrible* day," said Gianna, speaking up for the first time since they'd left the goat pen. "And all because I lost my lucky cap!"

Her mom squeezed her shoulders. "You don't really believe that, do you, Gia? You don't have good days and bad days because of what you wear on your head. You choose to *make* a day good or bad. It's up to you—and your attitude. Now, can you put on a happy face?"

Gianna tried to smile, but she ended up looking like Gloom, the stinkweed Pokémon with the sad face. In fact, Gia seemed to ooze sadness. Ethan had to look away.

"How about a peanut butter sandwich?" asked Mrs. Walker, digging in her tote bag.

"I'm not hungry," said Gia.

"Then at least drink some juice," said her mom, handing her a juice box.

Devin slid over on the bench next to Gianna. "You know, you're kind of like a butterfly right now," she said. "Did you know they don't eat either? They only drink nectar."

Here we go again, thought Ethan. *It's Devin the butterfly guide.*

His sister took a bite of her sandwich and then said, "Did you know butterfly smell with their antennae?"

Ethan couldn't take it anymore. "Devin, you're not supposed to talk with your mouth full. And you shouldn't talk about antennae. You're just reminding Gia about her lost cap."

Devin clamped her hand over her mouth. "Oh, sorry, Gia," she said.

Gianna shrugged. "It's okay. I like talking about butterflies. They smell with their antennae, and that's kind of what I do with my lucky cap, too. I sniff out Pokémon. Or at least I *used* to . . ."

She set down her juice box and slumped forward onto the picnic table.

"Alright, that's enough," said Mrs. Walker. "It's a beautiful summer day. We're all here at the zoo together. And there are things to do and see that have *nothing* to do with that cap. Don't you kids have a scavenger hunt to finish?"

"Oh, yeah!" said Ethan, glancing down at his shirt. "We only found two out of three stickers. Team Valor is still around here somewhere."

"Probably in the Primate House, with all the monkeys," joked Carlo.

He had been pretty down on Team Valor ever since they'd tried to take over Dottie's Doughnuts, his favorite Team Mystic gym in Newville.

"Yeah," Ethan agreed, "we should go straight to the ape cage to look for the Team Valor sticker."

"Actually," said Carlo, "maybe we *should* look in the Primate House—for real. Team Valor is all about strength and power, remember? And what's stronger than a gorilla?"

"Yes! Plus we get a prize at the gift shop when we're done, remember, Gia?" said Devin.

That perked Gianna up a little. "I hope the prize is one of those bug umbrellas," she said. "If I can't find my lucky cap, at least I can pop up a ladybug over my head."

"That's the spirit!" said Mrs. Walker. "Now, how about a sandwich?"

When Gianna took one, Ethan was relieved. Things were finally getting back to normal around here.

Team Valor, we're coming to get you, he thought to himself, taking a big bite of his own peanut butter and jelly sandwich. *Where is the primate house, anyway?*

He glanced over both shoulders, wondering which direction they should wander in next. That's when he saw the girl with the Caterpie cap—the one who lied about getting it in the gift shop!

But why did she lie? Ethan wondered. He followed her with his eyes as she walked toward the ice cream cart in front of the snack bar and the restrooms.

That's when he saw his opportunity. "I'm going to, um, use the restroom real quick," he said, excusing himself from the table. Then he darted toward the ice cream cart.

He was just about to tap the girl on the shoulder when he realized something. This wasn't the same girl at all. Instead of a long blonde braid, she had shoulder-length brown hair.

Ethan couldn't believe his eyes. Was there really more than one Caterpie cap floating around the zoo today?

He glanced back at the picnic table, hoping Gia

hadn't seen the cap.

Too late. She and Devin were already on their way over. Devin only had eyes for ice cream, but Gia's eyes were trained on that Caterpie cap.

"Where are they all coming from?" she asked, throwing her arms out wide. "Is someone playing a mean joke on me?"

"No!" said Ethan. "I'm sure there's a logical explanation. Remember the Team Mystic motto?"

"Sure. We calmly analyze every situation," said Gia flatly, quoting Blanche from the Pokémon GO game.

"Or we eat ice cream," said Devin, who had a wicked sweet tooth. She was already licking a peanut-butter-chocolate ice cream cone. "C'mon, Gia. They have cookie dough ice cream—your favorite!"

"Actually," said the man scooping ice cream from the cart, "we just ran out. Sorry, girls."

Ethan noticed that the blonde girl wearing the Caterpie cap was walking away with lumpy ice cream that looked suspiciously like cookie dough. He wanted to chase her down and grab it right out of her hand. That's Gia's ice cream!

But Gia seemed to be taking it all pretty well. Then Ethan saw that she was staring at something, or someone.

He followed her gaze—and couldn't believe his eyes.

Another pair of antennae bobbed along with the crowd. Only these antennae were *black*, and they were stuck to a purple cap with little white wings.

That's not Gia's cap, Ethan realized. *That's not even a Caterpie cap.*

That was a Butterfree cap.

It was as if the bug caps—and the mystery—were evolving right in front of his eyes.

CHAPTER 9

The Primate House felt dark and cool after the sunny picnic area. Ethan shivered and stuck his hands in his pockets.

The exhibit was one long tunnel winding around in a circle, past tree forts and jungle gyms showcased behind glass windows. Ethan wondered if the Team Valor scavenger hunt station was somewhere in the Primate House, but he didn't want to hurry past all the monkeys and orangutans.

"Look at that one!" he said, pointing toward a black-and-white monkey with a long, white tail.

"That's an Eastern Black-and-White Colobus," Mrs. Walker read off the sign on the wall.

"It's pretty cool," said Carlo, peering through the glass.

"It says that the Colobus monkey makes lots of different sounds," Devin added, reading the fine print on the sign. "It purrs, snorts, honks, roars, and screams."

"Sounds like you when you're sleeping!" Ethan joked. He had to duck quickly to avoid a punch in the shoulder.

"I like this guy even better," said Carlo, pointing toward the orangutan. "Look at how long his arms are!"

"Ooh, we can measure our own," said Gianna, pointing toward a measuring stick painted on the wall.

She leaned against the wall and spread out her arms.

"Okay," said Mrs. Walker. "From fingertip to fingertip, you measure four feet, two inches. That makes you closest to"—she checked the chart—"a gibbon."

That was the ape on the chart with the smallest arm span.

"I'm a smart gibbon, though," said Devin. "Want to know how I know?"

Ethan laughed. "Sure."

"Because I just spotted the third scavenger hunt

station. Let's go!"

Ethan followed Devin through the crowd. Just as they passed the chimpanzee cage, she slowed to a stop beside a table draped in red.

Sure enough, Team Valor had set up shop in the Primate House. Ethan turned around to give Carlo a high five. "We were right!" he said.

The woman standing beside the table gave them the whole spiel. "Good afternoon, kids. I'm Candela, leader of Team Valor. My team is researching ways to enhance a Pokémon's natural power."

Ethan was surprised she didn't roll up her sleeve and flex her bicep or something. "Do we get a sticker?" he asked, hoping to cut her off before she launched into a full speech.

"Not yet," she said. "First, let me share a few facts. Mankey may be a Fighting-type Pokémon, but the most *powerful* ape is actually the gorilla. Did you know a gorilla can lift ten times its own body weight?"

Surprise, surprise, thought Ethan. *Everyone knows gorillas are powerful.*

Then he saw something that was surprising. A chimpanzee was staring at him through the glass with sad, soulful eyes. And the chimp was wearing a hat.

A hat with antennae.

Ethan stepped toward the glass.

"Wait, you didn't get your sticker yet!" Devin said, calling him back.

Ethan reached toward the antennae, as if his hand could pass right through the glass. Then he realized the chimp wasn't actually wearing the cap. It was just a reflection on the glass.

Someone *behind* Ethan was wearing the cap. He whirled around and came face to face with a boy in a Beedrill cap.

"Seriously?" Ethan said out loud. "What's with all the bug caps?"

Candela, leader of Team Valor, stopped talking, and all the heads at the scavenger hunt table whirled around to face Ethan. Mrs. Walker looked at him, too, and raised her finger to her lips.

"Sorry," he said. "I just want to know where all the bug caps are coming from."

The boy wearing the Beedrill cap shrugged. "From the gift shop," he said. "Duh."

Ethan fought the urge to go all Mankey on the boy. He knew the caps weren't there. He had already *been* to the gift shop. But every kid wearing a bug cap at the zoo today couldn't be lying about where the caps came from.

Gia took one look at Ethan's clenched fists and

stepped toward him. "Calm down, Ethan," she said. "Remember the Team Mystic motto. How does that go again?"

Ethan took a deep breath. "We need to calmly analyze the situation. Right." *If Gia can be calm at a time like this, I can, too*, he told himself. "So, should we go back to the gift shop?"

"To the gift shop!" repeated Gia. "Let's do it."

"Wait!" Devin called. She was still standing by the scavenger hunt table with a miffed-looking Candela. "We didn't get our stickers yet."

Ethan wondered if the woman would still pass out the stickers, even though he had kind of interrupted her speech.

Luckily, she did.

So with their red stickers stuck beside their blue and yellow ones, Team Mystic marched back to the gift shop. The whole way there, Devin wondered out loud what their prize would be for completing the scavenger hunt. Ethan wondered instead where all the bug caps were hiding.

As soon as they stepped inside the gift shop, Devin hurried to the counter and showed off her sticker-covered shirt. "We completed the scavenger hunt," she announced proudly.

Ethan, meanwhile, took another pass through the aisles. He looked high and low for bug caps.

Were they hanging from the ceiling? Hiding behind the stuffed animals? Stuck at the bottom of a bin?

He searched *everywhere*—until Devin called him over to the counter.

"You get to choose one," she said to him. But her voice sounded very strange.

"One what?" asked Ethan.

He stepped around the corner of the counter to look in the plastic bin that the cashier had uncovered.

And there, laid out in rows in the long bin, were . . .

Caterpie.

Butterfree.

And Beedrill.

The prize for finishing the scavenger hunt was a bug cap.

Ethan didn't know whether to laugh or cry.

CHAPTER 10

Ethan chose the black-and-yellow Beedrill cap, but he couldn't quite bring himself to put it on his head. He noticed that Gianna was having a hard time even picking out a cap.

"Don't you want a Butterfree like mine?" asked Devin, sporting the purple cap with a smile. "I thought you loved Butterfree."

"I like *bugs*," said Gianna, crossing her arms. "I like my old bug cap. My lucky, old, bug cap. I don't see that cap in here, do you?"

"Gia," her mother scolded gently. "Don't be rude. Now, choose a cap so that the cashier can get back to work."

"Sorry," Gianna mumbled. She reached for a purple Butterfree cap and politely thanked the cashier, who put the lid back on the bin and slid it under the counter.

"Can we do some more shopping for souvenirs?" asked Carlo, pulling some money out of his pocket.

"Yeah," said Ethan. "My mom gave us money to spend, too!" He fished the money out of his pocket and passed a ten-dollar bill to Devin. Her eyes lit up, and she headed straight toward the plastic animal bin.

Surprise, surprise, thought Ethan. If there was something to collect, his sister was on it.

"Sure," said Mrs. Walker. "You can shop. But whatever you buy is going straight into the car. I'm not chancing another lost item today. Got it?"

"Got it," said Ethan with a grin.

Twenty minutes later, Carlo was wearing a silver pendant shaped like a polar bear claw around his neck. Ethan had his own sort of necklace—a long stuffed boa constrictor. Gianna had a ladybug umbrella popped open above her head. And Devin had a bag full of tiny plastic animals—one of every animal she could find in the display.

In Devin's other hand, Ethan spotted small bags of gummy bears and gummy snakes. "Did you spend your money on candy?" he asked.

She couldn't answer him. Her mouth was too full. She shrugged, swallowed, and then asked, "Do you want some?"

"No, thanks." He pretended to be disgusted, but he regretted that choice as soon as her back was turned. Those gummy snakes *did* look pretty tasty.

"Alright, kids, hand it all over," said Mrs. Walker, holding open her tote bag. "I'll bring your souvenirs to the car. Put your bug caps in there, too, please."

When the bag was full, she added, "You can wait for me out front. No wandering off to the petting zoo this time." She gave Carlo an especially stern look and then hurried toward the parking lot.

While they waited, Ethan settled onto a bench and pulled out his phone. "Any Pokémon sightings?" he asked Carlo.

"Just a boring little Weedle," said Carlo as he plunked down on the bench, too.

"Hey, can I play on your phone?" Gianna asked her brother. "I don't think Mom is going to loan me hers again anytime soon. Pretty please?" She clasped her hands together and gave Carlo her best puppy dog face, which reminded Ethan a little of Eevee.

Carlo shrugged. "Sure, but without your lucky cap, the zoo has pretty much run dry on the Pokémon front." He logged out and handed Gianna his phone.

She punched in her password and then asked, "So where is that Weedle again?"

"Walk toward the gift shop," said Ethan, waving his arm toward the front door of the building.

"Oh, yep! There it is. Thanks!"

"You seem awfully excited about a Weedle," said Ethan. "Those little Larrys are like my least favorite Pokémon."

"Same here," said Devin, popping another gummy bear into her mouth.

Gianna shrugged. "What can I say? I like bugs."

Then she shrieked and started jumping up and down. "I did it! I did it! I earned my silver Bug Catcher medal. Yes!"

"Good job!" said Ethan. "And all because of a Weedle?"

"It just takes one!" said Gianna, dancing around the bench. "Well, actually, it takes fifty. But the Weedle put me over the top."

"What's all this?" called Mrs. Walker as she hurried back up the sidewalk, her car keys jingling in her hand. "Are we celebrating something?"

When Gianna told her about the Bug Catcher

medal, Mrs. Walker looked pretty happy, too. "That's my girl," she said, kissing the top of Gianna's head. "We love our bugs, don't we?"

"We do," said Gianna, pulling up her Pokédex to flip through all the Bug-type Pokémon she'd caught.

"You caught a Butterfree, huh?" asked Devin, wiping her sticky fingers on her shorts before pointing at the screen.

Gianna nodded. "That was probably the most exciting bug I caught—well, that and Beedrill."

Then she grew quiet and started chewing her bottom lip.

"What are you thinking about, Gia?" Ethan asked. "Your battle with Beedrill?"

"No," she said. "I was thinking that I wish Mom had found that Blue Morpho that got out." She turned toward her mother. "Can we go back to the Butterfly House to see if they caught it yet?"

Mrs. Walker's face softened into a smile. "You bet," she said. "That's a great idea."

Yes! thought Ethan. The zoo wasn't exactly swarming with Pokémon right now, but the Butterfly House was at least full of PokéStops.

But as he pushed up from the bench, he saw the warning message pop up on his phone: BATTERY LOW.

Great, he thought. *Now I'll be stuck reading factoids with Devin.*

He turned off his phone and sighed. Then he jogged down the path to catch up with his friends.

"Look, there's Spark!" whispered Devin, pointing toward the gray-haired man with glasses. He was standing just outside the Butterfly House talking with another zoo guide.

Mrs. Walker corrected her. "His name is Mr. Thompson, actually. And he's very knowledgeable about butterflies. I'll go ask him if the Morpho has been spotted."

Ethan watched her approach the man. But after a quick conversation, Spark shook his head.

"Bummer," said Gianna, kicking at the dirt with her shoe. "I was hoping the Blue Morpho would be fluttering around back inside the Butterfly House by now."

"Or hitching a ride on someone's butt," said Devin with a smile and sideways glance at Ethan.

He fake-laughed. "Very funny." Then he fought the urge to actually twist around and look for the butterfly.

Gia gazed up at the sky. "Where could it be?"

she asked. "On a rooftop? In a tree?"

"I don't know," said Devin. "But I think I read something about where butterflies like to hide. It was on one of those little signs in the Butterfly House." She pulled out her phone and started swiping through her photos.

Great, thought Ethan. *Miss Butterfly Factoid is at it again.*

He looked around for Carlo, who was collecting Poké Balls at the PokéStop near the front door. Ethan started to check his own phone, and then remembered the battery was shot.

"Okay, I found it," said Devin, clearing her throat. "The sign said 'Some butterflies are nearly invisible. They blend into their surroundings, an ability called . . .'"

"Camouflage?" suggested Carlo.

"Yes!" said Devin. She kept reading. "'Many butterflies have wings that are bright on top and dull underneath. When they're in danger, they land on twigs or leaves and fold up their wings to hide.'"

Gianna tapped her chin with her finger. "So . . . we should look for twigs or leaves? But that could be anywhere!"

Devin shrugged. "I'm just telling you what I read."

Ethan sighed. "Where did we see the Blue Morpho?" he asked. "Where in the Butterfly House, I mean."

Devin laughed. "Smack dab on top of your head."

He stared at her for a moment. "I *know* that. But where were we standing?"

"By the bridge!" said Gianna. "It was right before the bridge over the stream, the place where I caught Goldeen."

"And almost fell into the water," her mother reminded her as she rejoined the group. "What are you kids talking about?"

"We were remembering that the Blue Morpho was by the stream in the Butterfly House," said Gianna. "Butterflies like water, right? So maybe we just need to look for water."

Her mother nodded. "Maybe," she said. "But I don't think there's a lot of water here at the zoo. It's mostly blacktop."

"How about the Polar Passage?" asked Devin. "There's water there. The polar bears have a pool, and the seals have a tank."

"I don't think the Morpho is swimming with the polar bears or seals," said Gianna. "It's a tropical butterfly, remember? Morphos like heat, not arctic air."

Ethan was barely listening. He spun in a slow circle, trying to remember where he had seen water—*real* water, not the kind in a tank or exhibit.

Then he remembered.

"The train! We crossed a bridge when we were on the train. The bridge went over a river!"

Carlo's face fell. "I'm not getting back on that train," he said. "You can't make me."

He looked so terrified of the tiny train that Ethan almost laughed out loud. But then Gianna started running back toward the train station. And even Carlo had no choice but to follow her.

CHAPTER 11

"It's for little kids!" Carlo protested when they reached the train station. "I'm way too big." He planted his feet on the blacktop, as if daring Gianna to try to make him move.

"We don't have to get *on* it," she said, sounding exasperated. "We just have to follow the tracks to find that stream."

"Well that's a relief," said Mrs. Walker, laughing. "If Carlo is too big, I'm too big for sure. But remember, Gia, we may not be able to go everywhere the tracks go."

Gianna spread her arms wide. "Can't we just try, though? For the Morpho?"

Her mother nodded. "We can try. For the Morpho."

Ethan grinned at Devin. His feet hurt. His legs hurt. And his phone battery was nearly dead. But Gianna was back in action, hunting for bugs—*real* ones this time. And that gave him the energy to keep going, too.

When the chugging train left the station, Team Mystic did, too—on foot.

"The train goes past the prairie," said Carlo, pointing toward a fenced-in field of golden grass.

It took longer to pass the prairie exhibit on foot, but at least there was plenty to look at. "See the bison?" asked Ethan. "Look at the horns on that thing!"

"It looks like a giant goat," said Gianna. "You wouldn't get in a pen with that, though, would you?" she asked Carlo.

He shrunk back in mock horror. "Nope. If a bison ever chewed up your lucky cap, you'd be on your own, kid."

Everyone laughed at that—even Gianna.

"Oh, what are those little critters?" asked Devin, pointing at something poking its head out of the ground.

"Prairie dogs," said Mrs. Walker. "Aren't they cute?"

"They almost look like little Pidgey!" said Devin. "Without the wings, I mean." She took a few photos as they passed, trying to catch the prairie dogs when their heads were *out* of the holes instead of inside of them.

Then Ethan noticed where they were. "I think I see the bridge up ahead," he said, shading his eyes. "Is that the stream?"

"Yes!" said Gianna, starting to jog.

They passed a few more prairie dogs and a bison who snorted, blowing a puff of dust off the ground at his feet.

As they got closer to the stream, another train was just beginning to chug toward them over the bridge. Carlo took a step backward, as if the train might snatch him up and make him ride it.

As soon as it passed, they hurried toward the banks of the stream. Trees arched overhead, filtering the sun. As Ethan walked through the dappled light, he took a deep breath.

It's peaceful here, he thought. *Like in the Butterfly House. The perfect place for a Blue Morpho to hide.*

He crossed his fingers, hoping one would land on his head any second now.

But no such luck.

He and his friends searched the bank of the stream, the wooden posts of the bridge, the trees overhead, and even the piles of twigs on the ground.

"If that Morpho is doing its camouflage thing, it's really good at it," said Devin with a sigh.

Gianna crouched low on the bridge, peering over the edge. "Are those koi?" she asked, pointing toward the golden fish in the water below.

"Way out here?" asked her mom. She stepped closer. "Well, yes, I think they are! How pretty."

This time, Ethan took a closer look at the koi. He didn't have a Goldeen on his phone to distract him. "Huh," he said. "They really do look like giant goldfish."

Then he heard the scraping sound of Gianna's foot slipping off the edge of the bridge. He jumped up in alarm. So did Mrs. Walker.

"Gia, honestly, are you determined to fall in today?" she asked, pressing her hand to her chest. "First at the Butterfly House, and now here."

Ethan waited for Gianna to crack a joke about her clumsiness, but she didn't. Instead, her face broke into a smile.

"Oh, mom," she said. "I could kiss you. You just reminded me of something!" She stood up and raced toward the end of the bridge.

"What?" asked Mrs. Walker.

Gianna was already running back toward the prairie. "You just reminded me where I left my bug cap!" she shouted over her shoulder. "C'mon!"

A flood of excitement filled Ethan's chest. He was about to follow Gianna. Then he watched his friend trip over a twig, fly through the air, and tumble to the ground.

"Ouch. That looks like it hurts," said Devin, crouching low beside Gianna. Her ankle was already swollen, and Ethan was pretty sure it was turning purple.

"It *does* hurt," she said. But she was still smiling. "Carlo, can you give me a piggyback ride? We have to get back to the Butterfly House!"

"Whoa," said Mrs. Walker. "Let's take care of your ankle before we worry about finding that bug cap."

"But where did you remember leaving it?" Ethan couldn't help asking.

"By the bridge in the Butterfly House! Because I almost dropped Mom's camera, and she told me not to drop anything, so I took off my cap and set it down. I remember now!" The words flowed out of her mouth like a waterfall. "Do you think it's still there? Am I actually going to get my lucky cap back?"

"I don't know," said her mother. "I'm more worried about how we're going to get you back—to the car, that is."

When she heard the sound of another train whistle, Mrs. Walker glanced over her shoulder.

Ethan knew what she was thinking before she even said a word.

So did Carlo. "I'm not getting on that thing," he told his mother. "I already told you."

But Mrs. Walker ignored him. As the train slowed to a crawl beside them, she waved and called out to the conductor. "Do you have room for a few more?"

The conductor must have seen that Gianna was injured, because he pulled the brake, and the train screeched to a halt. Ethan could see a few empty spots in the last car. He could also see Carlo inching away from the train.

"Let me help you get her inside," said the conductor, hopping out of the train. "That looks like a nasty sprain!"

Pretty soon, Gianna was settled into a seat. Devin scooted in beside her, and Mrs. Walker ducked her head to climb in, too.

"There's room for you boys, I think," said the conductor, reaching out his hand toward Carlo.

"Yeah, that's okay. I think I'll walk," said Carlo.

"Me, too," Ethan said quickly. He didn't mind the train so much, but he didn't want Carlo to know that.

"Suit yourselves," said the conductor, hopping back into the train.

"Go straight to the Butterfly House," Mrs. Walker called out the window as the train began rolling forward. "Don't make me come looking for you!"

Her voice was drowned out by the sound of the whistle. "That was a close one," said Carlo, pretending to wipe sweat off his brow. "Do you think we can beat them back to the Butterfly House?"

"Run, you mean?" asked Ethan.

But Carlo was already sprinting away.

"Hey, no fair!"

Ethan ran past bison and prairie dogs. He beat the train back to the station, and even managed to wave at Devin as he passed. But as he passed the Rainforest Center on his way to the Butterfly House, Carlo was nowhere in sight. Where was he?

There! He was already standing in front of the Butterfly House playing Pokémon GO. And when Ethan got closer, he could see that Carlo hadn't even broken a sweat.

So not fair, thought Ethan. *Carlo has longer legs. And his phone battery still has a charge.*

"What took you so long?" asked Carlo, grinning. "And why aren't you collecting Poké Balls?"

Ethan shrugged. "Dead battery," he said. "Or almost dead, anyway. What'd you collect?"

Carlo leaned over to show him.

Ethan recognized the blue Great Balls and the yellow, diamond-shaped Revive. "What's with the pink bottle? Is that a Super Potion?" he asked. Usually Potions were purple. But he knew that when a player got to Level Ten, they could start collecting more powerful Potions.

"Even better than that," said Carlo. "It's a *Hyper* Potion. It restores the HP of a Pokémon by two hundred points."

"Whoa," said Ethan.

"You'll get some too when you reach Level Fifteen," said Carlo.

"You're at Level Fifteen already?" asked Ethan. "I thought you were only at Thirteen!"

Carlo just grinned. "Stick with me, kid."

Ethan shook his head. *I'll never catch up to Carlo,* he thought. *No matter how much I play Pokémon GO—or how fast I run.*

Then he remembered why they were really at the Butterfly House. It wasn't to collect Hyper Potions. "Should we go in and look for Gia's cap?"

Ethan started toward the door, but Carlo wasn't

following him. "C'mon, Carlo. Let's see if we can find the cap before Gia even gets here."

When he turned around, Carlo was staring at him—or rather, at the top of his head.

Carlo slowly raised his finger to his lips. "Shh. Don't say another word. Don't move. Don't even breathe."

"Why?" Ethan whispered, his feet frozen to the concrete.

"Because," said Carlo, barely blinking. "You have a butterfly on your head, dude. A *huge* blue butterfly."

CHAPTER 12

"**W**hat do I do?" whispered Ethan. This was the third time he'd had a butterfly land on him today, but it was the only time it had happened when he wasn't in the safety of the Butterfly House.

If I make one wrong move, the Blue Morpho might flutter away and be gone for good, he realized. *No pressure there.* He felt his palms start to sweat.

"I don't know," said Carlo. "Just don't move." He glanced over both shoulders. "I wish my mom would get back here, or even Gia. But our two bug experts are on a kiddie train somewhere!" He seemed more disgusted with that train now than ever.

Ethan took shallow breaths so he wouldn't move his head. "Should I try to make it into the Butterfly House?" he asked.

Carlo chewed his lip. "Maybe. But first, let me go inside and try to find Spark. He'll know what to do. Remember, *don't move.*"

He tiptoed past Ethan and slowly pulled the first glass door open.

Ethan held his breath, hoping the movement from the door wouldn't scare the butterfly away. Then he counted the seconds, waiting for Carlo to return or for Mrs. Walker to get there—for someone to show up who knew what to do with a giant blue butterfly from the rainforest!

When he caught sight of his reflection in the window, Ethan almost laughed. *Who needs a Butterfree cap when you've got a real butterfly on your head?*

He spent the next sixty seconds fighting the giggles rising in his chest. *Don't move!* he ordered himself.

"Ethan!" someone called from behind.

He turned slowly, as if he were a fragile Pokémon egg suspended in an incubator. Then he saw Devin running toward him.

He wanted to scream at her to stop—or at least to slow down so she wouldn't scare the butterfly.

But if he shouted, he'd scare the butterfly away himself. So all he could do was hold out one hand and use his other hand to point toward his head.

When she was just a few feet away, Devin skidded to a stop and clamped her hand over her mouth. Then she turned around and ran back toward Mrs. Walker, who was pushing Gianna in a wheelchair.

By the time they reached Ethan, his neck had a cramp in it from holding his head so still.

"Try not to move," Mrs. Walker said.

"I wasn't planning on it," Ethan whispered. "But what do I do?"

"Wait till Mr. Thompson opens the door." She pointed toward the front door, which was opening ever so slowly.

Mr. Thompson, his eyes wide behind his thick glasses, was waving Ethan toward him. Ethan could see Carlo's anxious face, too, behind the second glass door.

"One step at a time," said Mr. Thompson. "You can do it, son."

Ethan had never moved so slowly in his life. It was hard just to lift his foot off the concrete, he was so afraid he would startle the butterfly.

As he walked, he kept his eyes on Mr. Thompson, who was staring at the butterfly. If it flew away, Ethan would know it just from the look on Mr. Thompson's face.

He took another step. Then another. And another.

Now he was standing inside the front entrance, between the two glass doors. As he let one door gently close behind him, he breathed a sigh of relief. *Halfway there,* he told himself.

Mr. Thompson guided him slowly through the second door.

Now, finally, Ethan was standing in that peaceful paradise. He felt the sun streaming down on him through the windows at the top of the Butterfly House. The Blue Morpho must have felt it, too, because that was when it took flight.

It fluttered its wings and floated up toward the sun. Mr. Thompson wandered down the path below it, talking to the butterfly as if it were his long-lost pet.

Ethan ran his hand through his sandy-brown hair and looked up. "I can't believe that was on my head," he said.

"I know, right?" said Devin, hurrying through the door. *"Again!"*

"Maybe your hair reminds the Morpho of a pile of dead leaves or twigs," joked Carlo.

"Gee, thanks," said Ethan. But he laughed. It felt so good to be able to move—and laugh—freely now without worrying about disturbing the butterfly. But someone was missing. "Where's Gianna?" he asked.

"She can't come in." Devin made a sad face. "The zoo had a wheelchair for her to use, but Mrs. Walker said it won't work on the stone path in here."

"Well," said Carlo, waving them deeper into the Butterfly House, "I guess we'll just have to find that lost bug cap for her. C'mon!"

They hurried toward the bridge, careful not to step on any butterflies. Ethan kept looking upward, wondering if his friend the Blue Morpho would be back. He saw Monarchs and Swallowtails, and even a Zebra butterfly fluttering past. But the Morpho had flown away.

"So where did she say she left it?" asked Carlo as they neared the bridge.

"I don't know," said Ethan. "She just said she put it down so it wouldn't fall into the water."

He searched the stone walkway and the wooden bridge. He even carefully stuck his head beneath the wooden rail and hung upside down, staring into the stream below. A big koi swam by, staring right back at him. But it wasn't wearing a bug cap on its scaly head.

"See anything down there?" asked Carlo.

"Nope."

As Ethan stood back up, he realized his sister had disappeared. "Devin!" he called. "Where'd you go?"

"Down here." Her voice was muffled by the plant she had crawled under. The leaves were long and green, like a giant umbrella.

Carlo laughed. "Are you playing hide-and-go-seek?" he asked. "Because, I can see you, you know."

"I'm looking for the cap," she said in a matter-of-fact voice. "It's green and yellow, right?"

"I think so," said Ethan. "I'm starting to forget, it's been so long since we've seen it."

"Well, if no one has found the cap yet, maybe it's because it's in a good hiding spot. It's *camouflaged*," said Devin, pronouncing the word slowly. "By something green. Like maybe a plant."

Ethan met Carlo's eyes and shrugged. "She could be right," he said.

As he dropped down to the ground beside his sister, an orange butterfly floated up.

Then he heard the squeal.

"It's here! I found it!"

Devin popped her head up out of the plant. Then her hand shot up, too—holding the bug cap.

"Yes!" said Ethan, reaching out to give her a

huge high five. "You found the lucky cap!"

"I can't wait to tell Gia," said Devin as she untangled herself from the long leaves of the umbrella plant.

"You won't have to wait much longer," said Carlo. "Look!"

They turned around, and there was Gianna hobbling toward them on a single crutch. Mrs. Walker held firmly onto her other arm, especially as they neared the stream. But they had both seen the cap. And they were both smiling widely.

Devin hurried over and gently placed the cap on Gia's head, right where it belonged. "There," she said, giving the cap a pat. "Now the Morpho butterfly and the bug cap are both home, safe and sound."

Gia laughed, which made the antennae bounce a little. "Thanks, Devin."

"I'd like to thank *all* of you," said Mr. Thompson as he walked toward them, his hands clasped. "Thank you for bringing that Morpho back where it belonged. I didn't think we were going to see our biggest butterfly again. I was worried!"

"We were, too," said Gia. "We're big fans of bugs and butterflies!"

Mr. Thompson reached out and wobbled one of her antennae. "I can tell," he said with a wink.

"Right now," said Mrs. Walker, "I'm worried about you, Gia. I think it's time to get to a doctor to check out that ankle. It's swelling bigger and bigger by the second."

"But, Mom! It doesn't even hurt anymore," said Gianna. "It must be my lucky cap working its magic."

"Oh, that's right!" said Carlo, pulling out his phone. "The Pokémon should start showing up around here again, now that the lucky Pokémon-catching cap is back on Gia's head." When his phone buzzed in his hand, he held it up and grinned. "See? A Venomoth. How perfect!"

"Really?" said Gianna. "Mom, can I use your phone? I haven't caught a Venomoth yet!"

Mrs. Walker shook her head firmly. "No. I think you have your hands full already," she said, nodding toward the crutch.

Ethan pulled out his own phone and turned it on, hoping there was enough juice left in the thing to catch the Venomoth. He didn't have one of those in his Pokédex yet, either.

It took a while for the app to load. By then, Ethan had just a smidge of life left in the red battery bar in the upper corner of his phone. But he barely noticed it, because something else had just popped up on his screen.

"Oh?" said Ethan, reading the screen.

It was an egg.

An egg that was about to hatch!

"My egg is hatching!" he said, nudging Carlo. "What do you think it's going to be?"

They both watched the egg crack. Then it cracked again. Then it wobbled.

But just as the Pokémon was about to spring out of the egg, something horrible happened.

The battery died.

And the screen went black.

CHAPTER 13

"**N**o!" shouted Ethan, staring at the black phone screen. "Not now!"

He shook the phone, knowing it wouldn't do any good. Then he turned toward Gianna, as if this were all her fault. "I thought your cap was lucky. Why would my battery die at a time like this? I was just about to hatch an egg. It doesn't get much more unlucky than that!"

Gianna bit her lip. He could tell she was trying not to smile. "You know what I always say, Ethan. You don't have good luck or bad luck because of what you wear on your head. It's all up to you— and your attitude. Now, can you try to put on a happy face?"

Mrs. Walker laughed. "What a wise daughter I have," she said, putting her arm around Gianna.

Ethan didn't want to smile, but he couldn't help it.

"That's better!" said Gianna.

It was a whole lot easier to smile when Mr. Thompson came back with a surprise for them. "I just talked with the zoo office," he said, "and we'd like to give you some free zoo passes so you kids can come back again another time. How does that sound?"

"Yay!" said Devin. "Count me in."

"Me, too," said Gianna. "But maybe next time, I'll leave my lucky cap at home. Right, Mom?"

"Oh no you won't," said Carlo. "Thanks to your lucky cap, I just caught a Beedrill with really high Combat Power. Two hundred and sixty-three!"

"Wow," said Ethan. "Yeah, Gia is definitely wearing her cap next time."

Mrs. Walker just shook her head as she led Gianna out of the Butterfly House. Ethan held open the door for them, making sure no butterflies escaped this time. He gazed upward and said a silent good-bye to the Blue Morpho, then let the door close gently behind them.

"You know," said Devin as they walked toward

the zoo exit, "we actually saw a lot more here at the zoo when we weren't catching Pokémon. Like those cute little prairie dogs."

"And the bison," said Carlo.

"And the koi in the stream," said Ethan.

"Oh, and don't forget the goat!" said Gianna. "You got an up-close look at that one, Carlo." She started laughing, but then winced. "Okay, maybe my ankle does hurt a little."

"We'll be at the car soon," said Mrs. Walker, holding Gianna by the elbow.

Devin walked on Gianna's other side. She couldn't really help her walk, but Ethan noticed how his sister tried to distract Gia by talking to her. *Devin's really good at that,* he realized.

"So you have two lucky caps now," she said to Gia. "Your bug cap and your Butterfree cap. How are you going to wear two of them at the same time?"

Gia shook her head. "No, I still have only one lucky Pokémon-catching cap." She almost reached up to pat it, then seemed to remember she shouldn't let go of the crutch. "But this one is kind of like a Caterpie. And Caterpie evolve into Butterfree, eventually. So . . . maybe I'll wear my Butterfree cap when I'm evolving my Pokémon."

"Or you could wear it when you're *hatching*

them," said Ethan. He couldn't stop thinking about his own Pokémon egg—the one that cracked open and then disappeared right before his horrified eyes. "Do you think my egg hatched already? Or will it crack open again as soon as I turn my phone back on?"

Carlo shrugged. "Only one way to find out. Luckily, Mom has a charging cord in her car. I bet it'll fit your phone."

"Really?" said Ethan, glancing tentatively at Mrs. Walker. He was afraid she would say no to more Pokémon playing in the car, but she didn't.

She nodded and smiled. "Sure. We'll give it a try."

A few minutes later, they reached her maroon minivan. Devin and Ethan slid into the way back, and Mrs. Walker pulled her seat forward to give Gianna plenty of room to stretch her leg out in the middle seat, too.

When Carlo plugged Ethan's phone in up front, Ethan held his breath. "Anything?"

"Not yet. You really drained your battery," said Carlo.

"I know! I can't stand it. Which Pokémon do you think was in that egg?"

Carlo shrugged. "I'm sticking with my first guess—Grimer." He spun around in the seat to give Gianna a warning look. "Don't even think about making a joke about the bubble gum on my shoe, either."

She shook her head and smiled, leaning back against the seat.

"I'm guessing it's Butterfree in that egg," said Devin. "Wouldn't that be funny?"

"Or maybe a Morpho?" piped up Mrs. Walker.

Carlo laughed. "Good one, Mom. Oh, look! Ethan's phone turned on." He unplugged it and handed it back to Ethan.

The Pokémon GO app started right up again. "But where's my egg?" said Ethan, trying not to panic.

He checked his list of Pokémon and sorted it by most recent captures. And there, at the top, was something new. Something yellow with an enormous snout.

When Ethan clicked on the Pokémon, it stood tall and wiggled its fingers at him, as if trying to cast a spell and lull him to sleep.

"A Drowzee!" said Ethan. "Cool. I don't have that one yet."

"Sure you do," whispered Carlo with a grin. "You have one right in front of you." He gestured toward Gianna.

Ethan craned his neck to see around the seat.

He could see that Gianna was nodding off to sleep. Her lucky bug cap sat cockeyed on her head, covering one eye.

He laughed quietly and then settled back into his own seat. A nap sounded pretty good, actually. What an exciting day! Team Mystic had solved not just one mystery, but two.

Team Valor may be strong, thought Ethan, closing his eyes. *But Team Mystic is smart. And we never give up.*

Do you Love pLaying Pokémon GO?

Check out these books for fans of Pokémon GO!

Catching the Jigglypuff Thief
ALEX POLAN

Following Meowth's Footprints
ALEX POLAN

Chasing Butterfree
ALEX POLAN

Cracking the Magikarp Code
ALEX POLAN

Available wherever books are sold!